Ghost Stories

Also by this author

Starsky & Kered's Adventures

Ghost Stories

Karen Evans

Copyright © 2018 Karen Evans

All rights reserved, including the right to reproduce this book, or portions thereof in any form. No part of this text may be reproduced, transmitted, downloaded, decompiled, reverse engineered, or stored, in any form or introduced into any information storage and retrieval system, in any form or by any means, whether electronic or mechanical without the express written permission of the author.

This is a work of fiction. Names and characters are the product of the author's imagination and any resemblance to actual persons, living or dead, is entirely coincidental.

The views expressed in this work are solely those of the author and do not necessarily reflect the views of the publisher, and the publisher hereby disclaims any responsibility for them.

ISBN: 978-0-244-36862-3

PublishNation
www.publishnation.co.uk

A Trip to Bodmin

'What shall we do today?' wondered Kaz out loud, switching the kettle on to boil.

Kaz has taken her nephew, Samuel, down to Cornwall for a few days visiting Samuel's Grandad Dave and Nanny Pat. At 5 years old, finding things to keep him entertained on a wet day can be a challenge.

Reaching to get some mugs from the cupboard, Dave said, 'Why don't we take him to that museum at Bodmin? It's not too far, and I think he'll enjoy it.'

Samuel has always been fascinated with the olden days. Even as a baby, it was only music from the 1800's that would soothe him – Beethoven's Moonlight Sonata being a favourite. So taking him to the Bodmin Jail museum would be ideal. Kaz was concerned that the mannequins depicting the crimes and punishments may be a bit scary, but decided that if Samuel got too scared, they could always leave.

The weather forecast looked like brightening up later in the day, so taking a picnic to eat on nearby

Bodmin Moor after visiting the museum seemed the ideal day out – combining history with a bit of fresh air.

After breakfast Dave loaded his car with a cold box full of food, a football, and some toys for Samuel, while Kaz struggled to get an excitable little boy dressed, deciding to keep where they were going a surprise.

As they pulled into the museum carpark, Samuel announced, 'Behind that wall just there, is a rope where they hung the naughty people!'

Exchanging glances, Kaz and Dave thought it must just be a coincidence as he couldn't possibly know that the hangman's noose was situated behind a wall in the carpark.

Entering the museum, Samuel headed off to the basement saying, 'If we're quiet, we won't be noticed.' Not sure what he meant, Kaz and Dave followed, stopping to read the plaques about the crimes and punishments from the Victorian era.

'Come on, hurry up,' whispered Samuel impatiently at his Aunty Kaz and Grandad Dave.

Wondering what the hurry was, they followed Samuel down into the basement. Surprisingly, they seemed to have the area to themselves with nobody else around. Maybe it's still early, thought Kaz.

Kaz and Dave were looking at the mannequins in the cells, depicting the crimes from the era, feeling very thankful that things aren't as harsh now as they were back then.

Wondering where Samuel had got to, Kaz went in search thinking he had gone very quiet.

On the floor which was set up as the work house for children and adults who had to work hard treading the wheel for water or picking oakum, often having to work 12 – 18 hour days as their punishment, Samuel was hiding in a dark corner facing the wall.

'Come on Sam, I can see you,' laughed Kaz, thinking that Sam was hiding from them.

Noticing that Samuel was shaking, Kaz went up the child and knelt next to him, wondering if it was too scary for him.

He looked up at her with fear on his face, and said, 'This is where we had to stand when we were naughty. My friend Thomas wasn't as lucky as me, he is still here.'

Looking around for her dad, Kaz wasn't sure how to respond to Samuel, wondering if they should leave.

Suddenly Samuel's face brightened and shouted, 'There he is!' and ran to one of the empty cells. Following him into the empty room, Samuel was chatting away to an empty space, as though he was chatting to a friend he hadn't seen in a while. 'Oh that's my Aunty Kaz,' said Samuel to thin air, 'she's brought me here on holiday to visit my Grandad and Nanny Pat.'

'Who are you talking to, Munchkin?' asked Kaz.

'This is my friend, Thomas, who I was just telling you about,' Samuel announced.

Wondering if Samuel was picking up on a spirit from the jail, which wasn't unusual as it was the sort of place where it was easy to pick up on the atmosphere, and she has herself experienced things there on previous visits, Kaz said to Samuel, 'Why is Thomas here?'

'Thomas stole some bread from the baker's because his family were starving, but he got caught! But it's ok because at least here he eats regularly and he has a bed to himself,' Samuel told her.

Going cold Kaz said, 'Come on, we ought to find your Grandad.' Walking out of the cell, Samuel followed her still chatting away to Thomas.

They found Dave, who was fascinated with the mannequins and the crimes in which people were punished for – such as stealing a loaf of bread or an apple to feed a family, as well as the more serious crimes which didn't bear thinking about!

Once they had finished looking at all the cells, Dave suggested getting a cup of tea and cake in the coffee shop attached to the museum.

Suddenly looking worried, Samuel stopped and said, 'But Thomas can't go with us into there, he'll get into trouble.'

Kneeling down, Kaz said to Samuel, 'Would Thomas like help going to his family or is he happy staying here in the prison?'

She explained to Samuel that if they helped Thomas to move on, Thomas would still be able to visit his friend and would be able to leave signs that he was around.

Without hesitation Samuel said, 'Please can we help him? He's lonely here.'

Kaz asked Samuel to tell Thomas to be brave and reassure him that he was going to be ok. Holding hands in a circle, Kaz and Samuel closed their eyes and asked for Thomas's family to step forward and make themselves known to Thomas so that he can go to them.

Feeling an overwhelming sense of love, Kaz saw a young lady with long dark hair wearing a shawl. Realising that this must be his mum, Kaz said, 'Its ok, Thomas, you can be free and at peace now.'

Going outside to sit in the warm sunshine with Samuel's Grandad, Kaz said to Samuel, 'How did you know so much about this place, Sam?'

Shrugging, Samuel looked up and saw a large white feather floating down from the sky and it landed at his feet – a sure sign from Thomas.

Kaz smiled, hoping that Thomas could now find peace, but realising that some things just can't be explained.

Christmas

'But I don't want to go to bed yet!' yawned Samuel stubbornly. It was 8 o'clock Christmas Eve night and Samuel was very excited about it being Christmas day the following day.

'Come on young man, bed!' said Samuel's mummy, trying to wrestle Samuel into his pyjamas. 'If you don't get to sleep soon, Santa won't visit.'

Struggling to keep his eyes open, Samuel reluctantly let his mummy carry him to bed.

'Which story would you like?' she asked, but Samuel was fast asleep almost as soon as his head touched the pillow.

Going back downstairs, Samuel's mummy poured herself a drink, thinking that she should have an early night herself, as it would be a busy day the next day.

Samuel suddenly stirred, hearing a jingle of bells. He opened his eyes and heard a loud THUD on the roof. Rubbing his eyes, he sat up in bed, and heard the bells again.

Going to his bedroom window to look out, Samuel looked in amazement as he saw that snow was falling.

'Wow!' Samuel exclaimed. He heard his daddy snoring in the next room, so knew his mummy and Daddy were asleep in bed.

It was dark outside, but Samuel was curious as to what the bells were that he heard. Creeping to the top of the stairs, he saw a glow of red and gold coming from the living room.

Sneaking downstairs to investigate, he pushed the door open and saw a kindly old man with a huge white beard sitting at the kitchen table eating the mince pies that had been left out.

Sensing that he had been caught, Santa looked around and winked at Samuel.

'Hello, you must be Samuel,' he said and held out his hand beckoning Samuel to go to him.

Nodding, not sure what to say, Samuel went and stood next to Santa.

'Thank you for my mince pies,' Santa said. 'They are just what I need to get me through the night.' He smiled. 'Well, seeing as you've caught me, how would you like to help me out? My reindeer are restless and I still need to deliver presents to all the children in the village.'

'What would you like me to do to help?' Samuel asked excitedly.

'Please can you feed them some carrots and keep them company while I finish off delivering the presents?' Santa asked.

Up on the roof, Samuel carefully fed some carrots to the reindeer, and looked in amazement at how far he could see, being so high up. All the houses were in complete darkness, except for the glow of red and gold where Santa was delivering his presents to all the children.

Samuel stroked the reindeers' noses in turn, softly talking to them to keep them calm.

Suddenly appearing next to him, Santa lifted Samuel into his sleigh, and then they were flying through the sky, laughing with delight.

Samuel looked in awe as they flew past all his friends' houses and by his Grandparents houses and his Aunty Kaz and Uncle Andy's house, waving and shouting 'Merry Christmas!' at each house in turn.

But then it was time to go home. Looking sad, Samuel asked, 'But will I ever see you again?'

'So long as you believe in magic, I will always be with you,' Santa replied before disappearing.

Waking up in bed in the morning, Samuel sat up, not sure if what happened was a dream or if it really did happen!

At the end of his bed, was a soft reindeer toy with a tag: 'To Samuel, thank you for your help last night, lots of love, Santa xxx'

Smiling, knowing that he had seen Santa after all, Samuel jumped out of bed and ran into his parents' room excitedly shouting 'HE'S BEEN!'

Running downstairs, Samuel pushed open the living room door and saw his presents.

'WOW!' he exclaimed.

Smiling, Samuel's mummy sipped her tea while Samuel opened his presents excitedly.

Hearing a faint jingle of bells from outside, Samuel stopped and smiled, knowing that he will always believe in the magic of Christmas.

Friends Day Out

'Can I help?' asked the Maître D, as Kaz, Lisa and Sharon entered the restaurant.

Kaz had booked a table at the newly refurbished restaurant within Bodmin Jail for a catch up with her friends.

'Booking under Evans,' advised Kaz, suddenly feeling very cold, despite the unusually warm evening. Following the Maître D to their table, Sharon and Lisa were looking around in awe, amazed at how beautiful the place was since being done out.

'So, what's the big news?' Lisa and Sharon said in unison to Kaz once they were seated, as Kaz had asked for a catch-up session with her two friends because she had something exciting to share.

'I'M GETTING MARRIED!' yelled Kaz excitedly, putting her hand over her mouth giggling when she realised that other diners had turned around to see who had shouted.

'Oh my God!' exclaimed Sharon and Lisa in unison, completely not expecting that news.

Kaz and Andy were always adamant that they would never get married, having been living together for over ten years, claiming they were happy and settled as they were.

'I know, I know, but with the money left to us from my Gran, we thought why not! Ideally we would go abroad, but then most of our family wouldn't go, so we're thinking of holding it here at Bodmin Jail now that they have a licence.'

Kaz's Gran passed away recently, and Kaz had a very close bond with her Gran and has received several signs from her spirit family, letting her know that Gran had passed over safely, so using the money left to her for something like this seemed the right thing to do.

'I can't believe it!' exclaimed Lisa. 'I honestly thought it would never happen.'

'Believe me, nobody is more surprised than me. We just decided on a whim and the more we talk about it, more right it feels,' replied Kaz.

Discussing plans and also each other's news while they ate, suddenly it was the end of the eve and time to leave.

Paying the bill, Kaz said, 'We're coming here tomorrow for a look around - why don't you both come, too? I'd appreciate my friends' opinion.'

Saying their goodbye's, Kaz, Sharon and Lisa arranged a time to meet the next day and went their separate ways.

Feeling a chill, despite it being a warm evening, Kaz put on her jacket and headed towards her car. Seeing a white feather on the passenger seat, a sure sign that maybe Gran has been with her all eve, which would explain the chill she was feeling, Kaz smiled as she got in and headed home.

The next day, Lisa and Sharon were waiting for Kaz and Andy in the coffee shop at Bodmin Jail as arranged.

'Hi guys,' said Kaz exchanging hugs with her two friends, suddenly feeling very cold again, despite the warm temperature outside.

Letting the bar staff know that she was here for her appointment, Kaz ordered coffee and cake while they waited.

Sitting down, Andy looked around, also feeling a chill, 'If it's this cold in here with it being so warm outside, we'll have to warn our guests to wear big coats,' he laughed, sitting down to catch up with Lisa and Sharon, drinking his coffee.

Suddenly, Lisa stood up. 'What on earth was that?!' she exclaimed.

Exchanging glances, Kaz and Sharon asked Lisa what was wrong.

'How could you have not heard that?!' said Lisa, shaking almost crying. Sitting down, Lisa managed to compose herself whilst she found the words to explain what had happened.

'Honestly, it felt like somebody shook the back of my chair and shouted 'Leave!' in my ear.' Realising how daft that sounded, especially as nobody else had seen or heard anything, Lisa went quiet and finished her coffee.

'You're just tired,' smiled Sharon sympathetically, concerned that her friend had been overdoing things recently.

'Perhaps you're right,' said Lisa feeling uneasy, but not wanting to ruin the mood for why they were there, she forced a smile and put the incident to the back of her mind.

Walking around the newly refurbished function rooms while the wedding planner spoke about numbers and figures, the girls and Andy looked around in awe, as the new owners of Bodmin Gaol had obviously spent a lot of time and effort into doing out the place, yet keeping it separate from the main Gaol.

'It's perfect,' muttered Kaz.

At the end of the visit, the wedding planner advised Kaz and Andy to call her once they had a date in mind, and she let them all through into the museum so they could have a good chat and a look around.

Shaking hands to say goodbye, Kaz said she'd be in touch soon and followed her friends through to the Gaol.

Kaz has a huge fascination with history and loved looking around the old part of the building.

They appeared to have the museum virtually to themselves. As it was such a lovely day, people were more than likely out making the most of the sunshine, which suited Kaz who wasn't fond of large crowds.

Suddenly getting goose bumps, Kaz put on her jacket, forgetting how cold it is in the cells.

'Kaz, here, quick!' called Sharon from a nearby cell.

Rushing to where Sharon had called from, Kaz suddenly noticed Lisa sitting on the floor shaking.

'Something literally pushed her,' said Sharon, her voice quivering.

'Lisa?' Kaz said, sitting down next to her friend, taking her hand. Lisa's hand was warm but shaky.

'I'm OK, honest,' Lisa stammered. 'It was weird,' she continued. 'I came into this cell and I honestly saw the shadow of a really tall man in the corner, and as I entered the cell and said "Hi" to him, he suddenly put his fist up and shoved me, but then disappeared into thin air.'

Wondering who it could be, Sharon and Kaz helped Lisa to her feet.

'I entered the cell just as she fell down and literally saw a black mist just disappear into thin air' exclaimed Sharon looking concerned.

'Are you hurt at all?' Kaz asked Lisa, but she shook her head

'No, just shocked, that's all. I wonder if it's the same person that shook my chair and demanded I leave earlier?' wondered Lisa.

Carrying on looking around the different cells, and shuddering at some of the punishments from the 18th century, the girls realised how lucky and easy they had it these days.

Catching up with Andy on the next floor, he called them over to a cell where two brothers had been imprisoned over killing a lady, and as neither brother would admit to the crime, both brothers were sent to prison and had a reputation for fighting.

'I wonder if this is who Lisa saw!' exclaimed Andy, realising that Lisa matched the description of the lady. 'He may have been trying to warn Lisa away,' he thought out loud with a shudder.

'OMG!' said Lisa now feeling uneasy.

'Maybe it's not a good idea having the wedding here,' thought Kaz. 'The last thing we need is Lisa being harassed by a spirit with a grudge to bear.'

Carrying on into the next cell, Sharon felt uneasy. 'There's def something not right, but I don't know what.'

'Come on, I have an idea,' Kaz exclaimed.

They all followed Kaz to the cell where Lisa saw the shadow man.

'No way am I going back in there!' shouted Lisa.

'Lisa, why don't you go and sit in the coffee shop and we'll join in a bit. I just want to try something,' said Kaz to her friend, giving her a hug.

'No, I'm staying, I need to let the brothers know they cannot scare me,' said Lisa.

Sitting in the middle of the cell, Kaz, Sharon and Lisa closed their eyes and held hands, imagining bright white light for protection, and imagining peace, Kaz asked the brothers to come forward.

Sharon was unsure about doing this, but trusted that Kaz knew what she was doing.

Suddenly the cell went almost pitch black, and they instinctively knew that the brothers were there.

Feeling Lisa shaking, Kaz gripped her hand tighter and imagined the bright light of protection to surround them further.

'Whoever you are, please leave my friend alone. She is not your lady, and we only mean you peace, not harm,' said Kaz forcefully.

'He's standing behind me!' said Lisa, her voice shaking.

'Be firm with him, Lisa. Tell him to leave you be!' Sharon shouted.

Taking a deep breath, Lisa shouted, 'You cannot hurt me. I am not scared!' Shaking, she sounded more forceful than she felt.

All three of them kept imagining the bright light to protect them, until eventually the blackness dispersed and the bad energy seemed to go with it.

Opening their eyes and standing up, the three of them noticed the cell seemed far calmer.

'WOW what happened?' queried Lisa in shocked amazement. 'Have they gone?'

'No, they'll still be here, but because you reminded them of the young lady they killed, you needed to let them know that they couldn't hurt you,' said Kaz, proud of Lisa for standing up to her fear of the unknown.

Having a group hug, they decided to go and join Andy in the coffee shop and discuss the wedding plans.

Linking arms they walked up the stairs feeling excited about planning the big day to come

Trip to Scotland

Kaz excitedly boarded the train bound for Aviemore, dropping her friend a quick text to let her know that she had boarded safely.

Kaz was visiting her friend who has recently moved to Aviemore. It had been a few years since the friends had met up, so Cal's recent move seemed the perfect opportunity to get together.

Settling down with a book, Kaz made the most of having the carriage virtually to herself and ordered a sandwich and some coffee from the buffet cart, then switched some easy listening music on to her MP3 to help her journey along.

'What book are you reading?' a kindly voice asked from across the aisle.

Kaz looked up, not realising further people had boarded the train and noticed a kindly older gentleman wearing a warm-looking tweed jacket and a matching trilby hat.

'I'm sorry, I didn't mean to startle you,' he smiled. 'You looked engrossed.'

Realising the gentleman was probably lonely, Kaz smiled and put her book down and stretched, not realising how engrossed she had actually got. And her eyes probably appreciated the break.

'It's a thriller set in the 1800's,' exclaimed Kaz. 'I'm fascinated with the history and also the punishments of that era. Gruesome, I know,' Kaz laughed, realising how odd she must sound to a complete stranger.

He smiled and went back to his paper.

Kaz decided to stretch her legs and go for a wander down the carriages looking for a toilet, and also maybe get a drink, realising she had let her coffee get cold.

'Can I get you a cup of tea while I'm up?' Kaz asked the gentleman.

Giving a wink, he smiled. 'I'll be fine with this, thank you,' showing his silver hip flask which was engraved with some sort of crest.

Smiling, Kaz went on down the carriage, stopping to make a fuss of an old Border Collie who reminded her of Starsky, her dad's old dog in Cornwall.

Returning to her seat some time later, Kaz noticed the gentleman had dozed off.

Leaning over to fold his paper up for him and making sure he was comfortable, Kaz went to her own seat and decided a doze seemed a good idea as it was still some time until she reached her destination.

Getting comfortable, Kaz put her headphones back in and settled down to relax and enjoy the rest of her journey, letting the vibration from the train rock her into a restful doze.

Waking sometime later, Kaz realised that they were close to Aviemore. Getting her belongings together, Kaz also dropped her friend Cal a text to say that she'll see her shortly and that they appeared to be on time.

Looking across the aisle, the gentleman smiled and wished her a good trip.

'Where are you staying?' he enquired.

'Oh, at the hotel opposite the train station,' Kaz smiled.

Cal had recently moved to a one bedroomed bungalow, so staying in the nearby hotel, which looked like an old-fashioned castle, seemed perfect, to allow each other space as well as for Kaz to fulfil her dream of sleeping in a castle.

'Do you have far to go? Is somebody meeting you?' Kaz asked, concerned for the elderly man.

He smiled, although this time his smile didn't reach his eyes. 'I'm a wanderer, don't you worry about me. It's time I came back home to my roots,' he said matter-of-factly. He tipped his hat and wished her a wonderful trip with her friend, and went off into the night.

As Kaz left the train herself onto the platform at Aviemore, she looked around but the elderly man seemed to have got lost in the crowd. Hoping he would be ok, she gathered herself together and saw her friend waving to her from the bridge.

Smiling, Kaz went to Cal, amazed that she had finally made it to Aviemore and excited about seeing her friend again and having a much needed catch up after so many years of corresponding over email and text and social media. It seemed surreal to finally be face to face.

Heading over to the hotel to get checked in, the friends chatted nonstop.

'WOW!' exclaimed Kaz as they entered the reception area, looking around in awe at the dark wood and the amazing staircase. It was just as she imagined a Scottish castle to look like from the olden days but with a modern twist.

Handing over the room key and explaining breakfast times and where her room was, the receptionist wished her an enjoyable stay with a warm smile.

'Go and get settled and freshened up, and I'll wait for you in the bar. Take as much time as you need,' smiled Cal. 'I'll make sure they have a bottle of Prosecco chilled,' Cal laughed, remembering her friend's favourite drink.

An hour later, Kaz was back in the bar, feeling refreshed from her sleep on the train and having had a hot shower and change of clothes in her room.

'This place is amazing.' Kaz yawned suddenly realising how very hungry she was, having only had a sandwich on the train. Kaz picked up the menu to have a look at what she could have and her stomach grumbled loudly. Laughing, Cal asked if she had a good journey. The two friends chatted over dinner and well into the evening.

When the bar man called last orders, the two friends were astonished that it was that time already, having chatted virtually nonstop. They finished their drinks and made plans for the following day. Kaz saw her friend off and headed up the staircase to bed shouting, 'Night!' to the evening receptionist as she passed.

The hotel had recently had a mini refurbishment and had put new beds in all the rooms. Kaz got into bed and almost immediately fell into a deep sleep.

During the early hours, Kaz woke and had an uneasy feeling that somebody was standing by her bed. Opening her eyes, Kaz sat up and saw a tall dark shadow pass by the full-length mirror at the end of the bed and pass through the door.

Switching on the bedside light, Kaz looked at her watch and saw that it was only just after 2 am. Feeling uneasy about what she had seen, Kaz switched on the kettle to make a hot drink and plodded into the bathroom to wash her face. Yawning, Kaz got back into bed with a hot drink and settled down with her book, wondering about what she had seen, knowing that it was the feeling of being watched which had woken her.

Unable to get back to sleep, Kaz decided to go and have a long soak in a hot bubble bath as she knew this would relax her, and decided to go down for an early breakfast.

After an amazing cooked breakfast and some strong coffee, Kaz noticed that the morning receptionist was just starting her shift, so Kaz went over for a chat.

'Morning, can I help?' enquired the receptionist cheerfully.

Kaz explained about her night time visitor and was quick to advise that she wasn't complaining, she is just curious as to who it could be.

Suddenly averting her eyes, the receptionist muttered, 'I'm sorry, but you must have imagined it. After all, you had such a long journey, you must have been very tired. Now if you'll excuse me, I really must get on,' and off she scurried.

Feeling bewildered by her reaction, Kaz went back up to her room to get her phone and handbag and sent Cal a text to let her know that she was ready when she was and felt excited about the day of sightseeing in a new place.

Enjoying the early spring sunshine, the friends took a walk taking in the views of the nearby Cairngorm Mountains, talking nonstop and enjoying each other's company.

Deciding to stop for a coffee and a sandwich at one of Cal's favourite bars, Kaz stretched and yawned. Concerned, Cal asked 'Are you ok? Did you not sleep very well?'

The fresh air combined with the very early start, Kaz realised how tired she had become. Smiling, Kaz assured her friend that she would be fine after some coffee and a sit down, and told Cal all about her early start and the receptionist's reaction.

'Maybe she's right, maybe I did imagine it, but it was just that feeling that somebody was watching me that I can't shake off, as up until that point I had slept soundly. It really did feel like there was somebody in the room with me.' Suddenly realising how she must sound, Kaz laughed and said, 'I'll be fine, it's probably just the excitement of sleeping in a castle, I've let my imagination run away with me,' and started tucking into her food.

Overhearing the conversation, the waitress clearing a nearby table recognised Cal as a regular customer and came over to say hi.

'Hi Jo,' smiled Cal warmly. 'I wondered if you'd be here today. This is my friend, Kaz, here for a few days' break.'

'Hi, lovely to meet you,' smiled Jo. 'I'm so sorry to interrupt,' Jo apologised to the two friends 'But I couldn't help overhearing your conversation. Which room are you staying in?'

'Room 11,' answered Kaz. 'Why?'

'I finish in about an hour. Can I meet up with you both later?' asked Jo.

'Of course,' smiled Kaz, looking towards Cal who was nodding her agreement.

'Listen, we're going to head back to mine in a bit, so why don't you come over when you are ready and you can join us for dinner as well, if you want?' suggested Cal.

Paying the bill, Kaz and Cal said goodbye to Jo and went back out into the sunshine, taking a leisurely stroll to Cal's place.

'Wow, this is lovely!' gasped Kaz, looking around Cal's new home. It was perfect for her friend.

'Go and sit in the garden, and I'll make coffee,' smiled Cal, pleased her friend liked her new home as her friend's opinion really mattered.

Pulling up a chair into the sunshine, Kaz sat down, taking in the scenery, feeling the most relaxed for a long time, the uneasiness from the night before forgotten.

Bringing out coffee followed by Savannah, Cal's newly adopted cat, Cal exclaimed, 'I can't believe how nice it is! You've obviously brought the weather with you.'

Not wanting to be left out, Savannah immediately jumped up into Kaz's lap, purring loudly. Laughing, Kaz made a fuss of Savannah who promptly curled up into her new friend and fell asleep.

Chatting away over their coffee, they made plans for the rest of Kaz's stay, and decided to catch the train into Inverness the following day.

Hearing the latch go on the gate, the friends looked up and saw Jo carrying lots of boxes.

'I thought I'd bring the leftover food from the bar for us to eat later. Be a shame for it to go to waste,' grinned Jo, taking it through to the kitchen.

Smiling, Cal followed Jo into the house to make more coffee. Savannah stretched, yawned and fell back to sleep in Kaz's lap.

Suddenly feeling a chill despite the sunshine, Kaz buttoned up her jacket and shuddered.

'So, how long are you visiting for?' asked Jo, bringing out a plate of muffins while Cal followed with a fresh pot of coffee.

'Oh, until the end of the week,' smiled Kaz, helping herself to a muffin.

'I hope you didn't find me rude earlier when I asked about your hotel room.'

'Not at all, I'm actually intrigued by why you asked,' Kaz smiled.

'Well, when the hotel was built in the early 1900's, it was designed specifically as a stopover hotel because of the busy train station across the road. The owner was my great-grandfather. The area where your room is now was originally the staff quarters,' explained Jo. 'The room you are staying in was his room.'

'WOW!' exclaimed Kaz and Cal in unison, both of them feeling goosebumps.

'So, do you think the shadow Kaz saw would have been your great-grandfather?' Cal asked

'I expect so. He wouldn't have meant any malice, just checking who was staying in his room,' Jo replied. 'I have a photo here somewhere, if you'd like to see it,' she said, going through her handbag.

'No way!' whispered Kaz visibly shaking when she saw the photo. 'This is the man on the train that I chatted with on my way here.' Going pale, she took in the friendly face and the same tweed outfit, then passed the photo to Cal to have a look.

'So, I wonder why the receptionist acted the way she did when Kaz spoke to her?' wondered Cal, passing the photo back to Jo.

'Well my grandfather had a sense of humour, and it appears that he sometimes likes to hide things or move things around in the staff areas and the staff sometimes get annoyed by it. The lady who was on reception this morning recently lost her ring but fortunately it turned up the next day, so as you can imagine, she wasn't too happy,' smiled Jo. 'So, tell me about the man on the train,' she turned to Kaz, noticing how pale she had become.

Kaz told her friends about the kindly gentleman on the train and how he appeared to just disappear into the crowd when they arrived in Aviemore.

'Well, he loved the trains so it would make sense that he would sometimes travel about on them. As far as I know, he hasn't been around in the hotel for a few months, so maybe he's intending on staying around for a bit this time,' Jo wondered 'He's obviously attached himself to you, and wouldn't have wanted to scare you,' Jo reassured Kaz.

Kaz smiled and the colour appeared to come back to her cheeks.

Bringing the food out that Jo had brought over, Cal picked Savannah up out of Kaz's lap so Kaz could move.

'This food looks amazing,' Kaz and Cal agreed.

'Perks of the job,' smiled Jo. 'We usually get to keep anything that doesn't sell, although it's not often there's this much.'

Chatting while they ate, they sat in the garden until well into the night, until tiredness got the better of her and Kaz made her apologies to get off to her bed.

'I'll walk back with you as I live that way,' Jo offered, hugging Cal goodnight.

Walking in companionable silence, Jo and Kaz walked along the main road towards the hotel.

'Thank you for tonight,' Kaz hugged Jo when it was time to part. 'I feel privileged to have met your great-grandfather.'

Opening her door, Kaz switched on the light and walked into the bedroom.

Briefly, out the corner of her eye, she saw the kindly gentleman from the train, who tipped his hat and smiled before disappearing into thin air. Smiling, Kaz waved goodnight and hoped that she would see her new friend again soon.

Printed in Great
Britain
by Amazon